Christmas in
HARMONY

Christmas in
HARMONY

Philip Gulley

HarperSanFrancisco
A Division of HarperCollins*Publishers*

HarperCollins books may be purchased for educational, business, or sales promotional use. For information please write: Special Markets Department, HarperCollins Publishers, Inc., 10 East 53rd Street, New York, NY 10022.

HarperCollins Web site: http://www.harpercollins.com
HarperCollins®, ♥®, and HarperSanFrancisco™ are
trademarks of HarperCollins Publishers, Inc.

FIRST EDITION

Library of Congress Cataloging-in-Publication Data has been ordered.

ISBN 0–06–052012–4
02 03 04 05 06 RRD(H) 10 9 8 7 6 5 4 3 2 1

To Joan, Spencer, and Sam—my best presents ever

CONTENTS

1. Christmas in Harmony 1

2. The Great Compromise 12

3. The Idea Takes Root 23

4. Preparations 34

5. The Unveiling 47

6. On the Verge 59

7. The Progressive 71

One

Christmas in Harmony

*M*y first memory of Christmas was in 1966. I was five years old and standing in line at Kivett's Five and Dime with my mother and brother, Roger, waiting to see Santa Claus, who looked suspiciously like Bud Matthews, the man in our town who did odd jobs. He smelled like Bud Matthews, too—a blend of Granger pipe tobacco, Old Spice aftershave, and sawdust.

For a while, I believed Bud Matthews was Santa, and that he spent the off-season in our town patching roofs and fixing screen doors. Bud Matthews was jovial, like Santa, and had a bushy white beard. His wife looked like Mrs. Claus on the Coca-Cola calendar at the Rexall. Except they had a son named Ernie, who was in my grade, and everyone knew Santa didn't have any kids, just elves and reindeer. Then

I

when I was eight, Uly Grant took me behind the school and told me that Santa was really your parents, which explained why, despite my persistent requests, I never got the Old Timer jackknife with a genuine bottle opener I'd asked for.

I needed the genuine bottle opener to open my pop bottles from Wilbur Matthews's garage next to the Dairy Queen. Wilbur was Bud's brother. I first met Wilbur at church. He was an usher and got to pick the boy who'd ring the bell to start the proceedings. I'd watch for his eye to settle on me and wait for his nod, which was the signal for me to slide out of my pew and fastwalk toward the foyer, where the rope dangled down from the bell.

"Pull her down a long ways," he'd say, "then let her go all the way back up. You'll get a good double ring that way."

The bell was made in 1885 in Baltimore. We got it cheap from the Episcopalians, who'd come to town in 1890 to establish an Episcopalian beachhead and convert the masses. But they folded after two years, and we Quakers bought it at their auction. Wilbur's grandfather had installed it, then had passed the bell ministry on to Wilbur's father, who'd bequeathed it to Wilbur, who was childless. These days, Dale Hinshaw rings the bell every Sunday morning at ten-thirty, just as the Lord intended when He caused the Episcopalians to be vanquished so we could have their bell.

It was Wilbur's custom to climb the ladder up to the bell every Christmas Eve and view the town's Christmas lights. If the night were clear, he could see the star on top of the silo at Peacock's farm, two miles east of town. In my seventh year, Wilbur let me climb the ladder with him. He pointed out the star. I thought it was the star in the East, that the Baby Jesus had been born in the Peacocks' barn. I wondered why the Peacocks hadn't invited Mary and Joseph into their house to sleep on the foldout couch next to the freezer in the mudroom.

Afterward, we'd retire to the basement and drink milk and eat Christmas cookies in the shape of angels Pastor Lindley's wife had baked downstairs while we were upstairs listening to him read the second chapter of the Gospel of Luke. The cookies were still warm and doughy, the milk so cold it hurt my teeth. If an angel head broke off while she was lifting a cookie from the cookie sheet, she'd put extra sprinkles on it and save it for me.

Pastor Lindley was a nice man, but seldom caused our faith to soar to new heights. If we wanted inspiration, we watched the Reverend Rod Duvall from Cleveland on Saturday nights after Lawrence Welk. We kept Pastor Lindley on because of his wife. We couldn't imagine tromping downstairs on Christmas Eve and eating hard, cold, store-bought cookies that crunched like gravel when you bit into them.

Though he was nice, Pastor Lindley had a few alarming tendencies, chief among them his sermons encouraging us to remember the reason for Christmas—that it wasn't about presents and cookies, but about God sending his Son to be with us. I feared my parents might take his message to heart. I had nightmares about running down the stairs on Christmas morning to a tree with nothing under it, and my father sitting in his chair, a Bible balanced on his lap, smiling and saying, "Your mother and I have decided that this year we're just going to thank God for the gift of his Son, because that's the only gift we really need."

The Christmas Eve service was, and still is, held at eleven-thirty. If we timed it right, we'd be biting into the cookies just as the Frieda Hampton memorial clock bonged midnight. My first four years, I came attired in pajamas, wrapped in a blanket, and slept through the entire proceedings. By my fifth year, my parents said I was big enough to stay up. I nodded off through the Gospel of Luke, but revived in time to eat cookies, which is my pattern to this day.

I have other memories of Christmas in Harmony. The men from the street department hanging plywood angels on the lightposts around the square. The Odd Fellows Lodge stringing Christmas lights back and forth across Main Street. The volunteer fire department hosing down the basketball court at the park so when it froze we could slide on the ice. Sorting through the pine trees at Grant's Hardware to find one with four good sides. Joe Bryant, who was a Jehovah's Witness and didn't believe in Christmas, telling me I was going to hell for celebrating it, but sneaking over to my house on Christmas afternoon to play with my toys.

Next to Christmas, the day before the holiday break from school was the best day. We'd play games in the morning and sing Christmas carols in the gym with Mrs. Rogers, the music teacher. At lunch, Mrs. Sisk, the school cook, would serve us green ice cream in the shape of Christmas trees. After lunch, we'd march two abreast out the school door and up Washington Street to the Royal Theater and watch *Old Yeller* or *The Jungle Book*. We'd walk out of the dark into the sunlight, blinking our eyes. When Pastor Lindley read from Isaiah how people who walked in darkness had seen a great light, I thought he was talking about the movies.

A lot has changed in my hometown over the past forty years, except Christmas. Plywood angels still flutter among the lightposts. Christmas trees still lean in rows outside Grant's Hardware. If the weather is clear, Dale Hinshaw can spy the star atop the Peacocks' silo. But Pastor Lindley moved away in 1970. Then Pastor Taylor came and stayed thirty years until he died. Now I'm the pastor and on Christmas Eve I stand and read from the second chapter of

Luke and encourage people to remember the reason for Christmas, that it isn't about presents and cookies, but about God sending his Son to be with us. Children all over the meeting room look up, alarmed. Then I read from Isaiah how people who've walked in darkness have seen a great light. The children nod knowingly.

There have been a few deviations over the years. In 1976, Dale Hinshaw, flexing his political muscle as chief bell ringer, had the church hold a traveling Nativity scene. The idea was to put the Holy Family on the back of Ellis Hodge's hay wagon, along with the shepherds, wise men, and a scattering of livestock. Then Ellis was to pull them down Main Street, past Kivett's Five and Dime, as a witness to pagan consumers who had forgotten the true reason for Christmas.

Dale had asked the stunning Nora Nagle, the state Sausage Queen of 1975 and daughter of church usher Clevis Nagle, to wear a bathrobe and play the part of Mary. But he'd failed to specify what kind of bathrobe and, while standing in front of Kivett's, was horrified to see the mother of our Lord ride past in a gauzy, slinky dressing gown.

I was fifteen years old and playing Joseph, the husband of Mary and stand-in father of our Lord. I was wearing my father's plaid bathrobe, as Dale had instructed. Ellis Hodge downshifted as we approached Kivett's, per Dale's instructions to linger in the area, giving nonbelievers sufficient time to be convicted of their sin. But the renunciation of sin was not the first thing that came to mind when they saw Nora Nagle in her dressing gown. The men along the sidewalk began to whistle, while I, her faithful husband, gazed adoringly at my betrothed, thanking the Lord for using me to bring Truth to the unwashed masses. The next year, we returned to the Gospel of Luke and cookies in the basement.

I left town after high school, and lived away for twenty years attending college and seminary, getting married, having two sons, and pastoring a church in the next state over. But every Christmas would find me home, sleeping in the bedroom I'd shared with my brother, doing what we'd always done. Eating potato soup at seven o'clock, visiting with neighbors, then walking the three blocks to the meetinghouse for the Christmas Eve service, my mother prodding us to arrive early and get a good seat, which mystified me, since everyone always sat in the same pew anyway.

It was a comfort to have this one steadiness, this unchanging center, in my life. I knew no matter what else changed, I could always count on hearing the second chapter of Luke read at Harmony Friends Meeting on Christmas Eve. I would sit with my eyes closed, letting the words wash over me. "And it came to pass in those days, that there went out a decree from Caesar Augustus that all the world should be taxed. . . . And she brought forth her firstborn son, and wrapped him in swaddling clothes, and laid him in a manger, because there was no room for them in the inn. . . . Fear not: for, behold, I bring you good tidings of great joy, which shall be to all people."

During the pauses, I could hear the pastor's wife down in the kitchen, sliding the cookie sheets into the oven, assisted by the Friendly Women's Circle after Pastor Taylor's wife rebelled. The smell of cookies would float up the stairwell into the meeting room, as the shepherds were abiding in the fields, keeping watch over their flock by night. By the time they came with haste to Bethlehem, the cookies were browning nicely. A few moments would be allowed for the shepherds to glorify and praise God for all the things that they had heard and seen, and then we would tread downstairs, just as the cookies were pulled from the oven.

One Christmas, on the verge of a midlife crisis, Pastor Taylor read from a Bible he'd ordered from California. "About that time, the guy in charge, King Augustus, ordered everyone to pay taxes or else. . . . And Mary had a baby and dressed him pajamas, and laid him in a garage, because the guest bedroom was being used. . . . And the angels said to them, 'Don't worry. Be happy.'"

But people weren't happy, not happy at all to hear their

beloved King James Bible trifled with, and there was talk of letting Pastor Taylor go. Three months later, he took up jogging, was struck by a truck, and died, thereby ensuring his reputation as a saint, his flirtation with modernity forgiven.

I was between churches and agreed to become their pastor, a decision I regret at least once a month during the elders meetings with Dale Hinshaw. The other twenty-nine days of the month, I enjoy being pastor. I especially like December, when we skip the elders meeting altogether.

When I was a child, Dale Hinshaw didn't seem any different from the other men I knew, who also wore plaid shirts, ate at the Coffee Cup, and complained about the politicians in Washington ruining the country. My father would occasionally mutter under his breath about Dale. At night, I would lie in bed, press my ear to the heating duct next to my bed, and listen to my parents talk about his eccentricities. Still, since all adults struck me as peculiar, I wasn't inclined to think Dale was singularly odd.

Then I became his pastor.

My first week in the job, Opal Majors stopped by to advise me, in a charitable sort of way and not meaning to gossip, that Dale Hinshaw was a few notes short of a song. "He has some rather unusual ideas," she said. "I'm sure he means well. But he watches television preachers and gets these kooky ideas."

"Like the traveling Nativity scene?" I asked.

"Yes, and bringing in Mohammed the Baptist and his camel for a revival. Camel poop everywhere. You should have seen it. What a mess that was."

I chuckled at the memory. "I didn't know Dale was behind that."

"Oh, yes. And don't forget Brother Bruno. Dale saw him on TV and just had to have him come here. Christian, my foot. The last night he preached, he made off with the offering."

"Say, I remember him. Wasn't he the guy from New York who'd been with the Mafia and found the Lord in prison?"

"That's what he said. We found out later he was a common thief. He and that Reverend Rod Duvall had a racket going."

"The Reverend Rod Duvall from Cleveland?" I asked. "The one on TV who wore a red, white, and blue suit, whose wife had pink hair and cried a lot?"

"One and the same."

"I never knew he was a crook."

"Rotten to the core," Opal said. "Turns out he was also selling illegal bonds. The IRS nailed him." She smacked my desk with her hand. "Squished him like a bug. Anyway, bringing him here was all Dale's idea, and I just thought you should know, now that you're our pastor."

The next few days saw a steady stream of parishioners to my office, each of them bearing a matter of great concern.

Bea Majors confided that she'd seen Asa Peacock buy mouthwash with alcohol in it.

Dale Hinshaw wasn't sure, but he'd heard Mabel Morrison was a vegetarian and had voted Democratic in the last election.

Eunice Muldock knew for a fact Uly Grant's wife was a shoplifter.

They weren't gossiping, they assured me, just sharing concerns I might wish to pray about, now that I was their pastor. I thanked them for their interest and told them I'd be sure to speak to the persons involved in order to convey their loving concern. "I'll be sure to mention your name so they know you care," I promised.

No thank you, they said, they didn't do it for the recognition, they just wanted to be of service. Naturally, I was pleased to find myself the pastor of such a caring fellowship, and looked forward to many years of ministry with these modest, prayerful saints.

In this unsettled world, it is good to have this steadiness—the Christmas Eve service, the peal of the bell, the star atop the Peacocks' silo, the saints burdened with concern. There is a holiness to memory, a sense of God's presence in these mangers of the mind. Which might explain why it is that the occasions that change the least are often the very occasions that change us the most.

Two

The Great Compromise

Our annual argument began the week before Thanksgiving, when the first Christmas card arrived at our home. "By the way," my wife, Barbara, said, "I'm not doing Christmas cards. If you want them sent, you'll have to do it."

She'd said that every year of our marriage, so I wasn't gravely concerned. I stopped past Kivett's Five and Dime that afternoon. The Christmas cards were stacked next to the sleds and snow shovels, up front by the gumball machines. I bought four boxes and laid them on our dining-room table along with the address book, hoping to nudge her along.

They sat unopened for a week. I moved them to our bedroom and laid them by her side of the bed. The next day, they had been moved to my side. She'd written *I WASN'T KIDDING* in big letters on the top box of cards.

This was my first clue that Christmas was no longer the benevolent holiday I'd loved as a child.

Cards began stacking up on our dining-room table, sent mostly by people from the church. I would open the cards, read them aloud, and comment on the sender's thoughtfulness. "Oh, and here's a special card just for pastors, from Opal Majors." I turned the card over, read the back, and whistled. "Two dollars and seventy-five cents, and her on a fixed income, and so crippled with arthritis she can barely write. Wasn't that sweet of her?"

"Yes, it was. And since you're her pastor, I think you should send her a Christmas card and tell her so," my wife countered.

I sat quietly, unable to think of a rebuttal.

Christmas, it occurred to me, had become a veritable minefield. If I didn't send Opal a card, she'd be hurt. If I sent her a card, she'd tell everyone else in the church, and they'd wonder why I hadn't sent them one.

I remember when my biggest decision at Christmas was what to buy with the ten dollars my grandparents gave me. The week before Christmas, my grandmother would walk up Marion Street to Vernley Stout's window at the bank, where he would count out two crisp ten-dollar bills, one for

Roger and one for me. She would arrange them in the money envelopes so that Alexander Hamilton's face peered from the oval window with grim concern, silently admonishing the recipient to spend him wisely, and not blow him on candy.

Alexander Hamilton seemed the picture of frugality. I would have preferred a fifty-dollar bill, with Ulysses S. Grant and his hippie beard, urging me to whoop it up. Unfortunately, Vernley Stout and my grandmother were disciples of Hamilton.

"Why don't you bring those boys down and we'll start a college account for them," he'd advised. "You'd be surprised how quick it adds up." My grandmother made us save two dollars each Christmas. By the time I went to college, I'd saved thirty-two dollars and seventy-eight cents under the fiscal guidance of Vernley Stout.

The other eight dollars were mine to do with as I pleased. Each year my mother would hint that I should give 10 percent to the work of Christian missionaries, which would have knocked down my take another eighty cents.

"For crying out loud," my father told her, "let the boy have his money. He'll be giving it all to the government soon enough anyway."

"Well, it's your decision, Sam," she'd say. "I just think it would be a nice gesture, that's all."

I decided to let the missionaries fend for themselves.

Eight dollars was big money in those days, when a candy bar cost fifteen cents and the Saturday matinee at the Royal Theater was fifty cents. Still, with a little determination, I could run through the whole eight dollars in one day. My brother, Roger, was a saver, like my grandmother. He'd put the whole ten dollars in his college account, which pleased Vernley and my grandmother to no end.

Vernley kept my grandmother's picture taped inside his teller's booth—a pinup girl for frugality. She began each day reading "Hints to Heloise," discovering myriad uses for worn-out hosiery, vinegar, and baking soda. Once, while nosing around in her kitchen pantry, I found a box labeled *String too short to use.* Every Christmas she would send the cards she'd received the year before back to the very people who'd sent them. She'd add her name below theirs, and write, *We return your greetings and wish you a Merry Christmas.* She'd written up the idea and sent it to Heloise as a hint, under the pseudonym Cautious Christian.

Caution was her byword. Another Great Depression was looming around the corner. She knew it. The house would be lost in a tax sale. Anarchy would follow, with war and pestilence close behind. Vernley had told her so himself. "The Christmas Club is your safest bet," he'd advised. "Two and a half percent compounded annually, guaranteed by the president of the United States himself." That the president was Richard Nixon didn't seem to trouble her.

My grandfather observed this with some detachment, spending most of this time out in his workshop in the barn behind their home. He'd wanted to tear down the barn and build a garage, but my grandmother wouldn't stand for it. "You watch and see," she'd said, "when hard times come we'll be back to riding horses and you'll thank the Lord for that barn."

On Christmas afternoons, my mother would send Roger and me out to Grandpa's workshop to thank him for our ten dollars. He would return our acknowledgment with a solemn nod, then return to his puttering. He smelled like oil and turpentine and was a hard man to get to know. I often had the feeling he'd rather be somewhere else.

He died the week after Thanksgiving my first year at college. My grandmother rang the bell outside their back door for lunch, then went back in and was halfway through her sandwich before she realized he wasn't seated across from her. She found him slumped over the push mower, a wrench in his hand. Johnny Mackey at the funeral home speculated that the strain of freeing a rusted bolt had done him in.

It fell to my father and me to clean out his workshop. I was sorting through a box marked *Lawnmower parts,* when I heard a cough, then a sob. My father was standing by the workbench, his back turned to me, crying. I'd never seen him cry before, and wasn't sure what to do. I went and stood by him and laid my hand on his shoulder.

He spoke in a muffled voice. "All these years, all I wanted was for him to tell me he loved me, that he was proud of me, and he never did. And now he never can. It was the only thing from him I ever wanted."

This was odd talk coming from my father, who'd never seemed inclined toward such sentiments. He pulled a handkerchief from his pocket, blew his nose, wiped his eyes, and then looked at me. "I don't ever want you to feel this way. I want you to know I love you, son. I'm proud of you, awful proud of you. Have been since the day you were born." Then he hugged me. It was the best Christmas present he ever gave me, those words.

Fast-forward twenty years: I have sons of my own. I'd taken them with me to Kivett's Five and Dime that day to buy more Christmas cards. The first four boxes weren't enough. They noticed the Christmas decorations and have talked of little else since. When I tucked them in bed, Levi, my older, asked, "What's the best present you ever got?"

I think back to that day in my grandfather's workshop. "Something my daddy gave me a long time ago."

"Will you give us one?" they asked.

"I do every night when I tuck you in," I said.

"What is it?"

"Someday, when you're all grown up with kids of your own, you'll know."

"Is this a riddle?" Levi asked.

"No, it's just a gift you get when you're little whose value you don't appreciate until you're old, like me."

"I think I'd rather have a pocketknife," Levi said.

"Nope. You'd poke your eye out. Now sleep tight. And remember your daddy loves you both."

"We love you."

"Proud of you boys."

"Proud of you, Daddy."

I walked downstairs and sat at the dining-room table to address Christmas cards. My wife and I had forged a Christmas-card compromise. I would write the inside, she would write the outside, and I would lick the stamps. We were working our way through the church directory, and were up to Vernley Stout, who wasn't even a member of our church, but in 1978 had attended a worship service and in a reckless moment dropped a check for five dollars in the collection plate, thereby gaining a place in our directory in perpetuity.

The standard for inclusion in the Harmony Friends Meeting directory is modest. Every person who has ever joined the church, attended worship, or even walked past the meetinghouse is listed. Even if they've forgotten they did. Efforts to remove a name from the rolls are met with determined resistance, as Fern Hampton documents their tenuous connection to the church. "Now that person there, I know she hasn't been here in a while, but I still get a letter from her cousin every Christmas, and I don't think we oughta kick her out just yet. Besides, didn't she send us three dollars last year to pay for her newsletter postage?"

This is the cue for Dale Hinshaw to clear his throat, rise to his feet, and suggest that *everyone* in the church should be removed from the membership list until they can prove they love the Lord. "First, I think they oughta be able to name all the books of the King James Bible, tell us exactly when it was they became a Christian, and show us their W-2 so we can see if they're tithing. Then, I think at the very least we oughta do some kinda background check, just to make sure we aren't lettin' in any liberals or perverts."

Several men in the church applaud Dale's suggestion, knowing this plan will cut their Christmas card list down to nothing. But Fern is scandalized at the thought the church might revoke her membership. She begins to weep, recalling how she has been a member of the church since she was a baby, and what would her mother think (may she rest in peace) if she looked down from heaven to see them removing her daughter's name from the church rolls, and how she was on a fixed income and maybe couldn't give as much money as certain other members, but that she'd like to think the gift of her time counted for something.

This is an oft-repeated drama that ends with Bea Majors standing in the second row and suggesting that no one there, not one person, was qualified to judge who was a true member of the church and who was not. "I may not know all the books of the Bible," she says, shooting Dale a look, "but I know it says in there somewhere about not judging, and I think that's exactly what's going on here, if you ask me."

The men begin to pray quietly for Dale to remain strong in the heat of battle, but he withers under Bea and Fern's two-pronged attack. He concedes defeat, and we resign ourselves to sending out even more Christmas cards. Fern Hampton, flush with victory, stands. "As long as we're on the topic of the directory, I'd just like to say that Judy Iverson's mother came to our Chicken Noodle Dinner and helped wash dishes. I think it would be nice to add her name to our directory."

And so our ranks swell.

"One hundred and seventy-eight cards this year," my wife said, as she addressed the last of our Christmas cards. "Who's Otto Zumwalt?"

"He fixed the freezer at the church."

"Why is the freezer repairman in our church directory?"

"The Friendly Women's Circle nominated him for honorary membership. They had a freezer full of noodles and it conked out. Otto had it up and running in two hours. Didn't lose a single noodle."

She opened the card and read my greeting. "'We love you'? Why'd you write that? Don't you think that's being overly familiar? He just fixed a freezer, after all. It wasn't even our freezer."

"I thought he might like to hear it," I said.

"Who else did you tell we loved them?"

"Well, uh, let me see, pretty much all the cards."

"Whatever happened to 'Merry Christmas'?"

"That's so, I don't know, traditional."

"It's Christmas," she said. "We're supposed to be traditional. 'Merry Christmas,' 'Happy Holidays,' or 'Thinking of you!' 'Sam, Barbara, Levi, and Addison.' They open the card, read it, smile, are glad we thought of them, and then they pitch it in the trash. Now you had to go tell them we loved them. It'll confuse them."

"What do you mean confuse them?"

She sighed. "Telling someone you love them changes everything. They'll think we're better friends than we are, and the next thing you know they'll be inviting us over for supper. Then we'll have to invite them over, and before long we'll be worn out. You don't say I love you to just anyone. It can get you in trouble."

"I'm beginning to see that," I said, chuckling.

"Oh, sure. Go ahead and laugh. But while you're being Mr. Loverboy, I'm the one who has to cook the pot roast and clean the house when Dale Hinshaw comes to visit his new best friends."

There is no calamity that can't be blamed on someone else, and I neatly turned the tables. "If you'll remember, I suggested you do the Christmas cards, but you refused."

"Are you saying this is my fault?"

"A reasonable person might conclude that, yes," I pointed out.

It is a sweet argument for us, repeated every year in early December. My wife, modest and traditional, argues for reserve, while I, having witnessed the pain of unspoken love, elect to splurge. It is, I believe, in keeping with the season. God could have sent a lawyer who would scrupulously define the limits of love. Instead, he went for broke, and sent a child with whom He was well pleased. And had the good sense to tell him so.

Christmas, I tell my wife, is not the time to hold back. It is the bold stroke, the song in the silence, the red hat in a gray-suit world.

Three

The Idea Takes Root

With the Christmas cards stamped and mailed, I could now direct my attention to the real purpose of Christmas, which was to make sure we didn't repeat the dreadful mistake from the year before, when a hundred and thirty-five people crammed our pews for the Christmas Eve service. We had been expecting our usual ninety-three and had failed to carry up folding chairs from the basement. The old-timers walked in, saw the hordes of people sitting in their pews, and were appalled. Pews, which had been in their family for generations, now occupied by total strangers! Fern Hampton fainted on the spot, and only regained consciousness after being stretched out on her pew and inhaling the fragrance of Hampton sweat, which after eighty humid, Indiana summers now permeated the pew. She sat up, blinked her eyes, and said, "Who in the world are these people and who invited them?"

Inquiries were made and meetings held, where it was determined the culprits were Miriam and Ellis Hodge, who'd had the gall to invite guests to the Christmas Eve service without instructing them to bring their own chairs. As for the cookies, the Friendly Women's Circle had to lop them in half to have enough. Baked to perfection and beautifully decorated, the angels underwent tearful amputation, halos and heads on one plate, wings and skirts on another.

It took many months for passions to cool. Then at the September elders meeting, Fern Hampton revisited the subject. "Well, I just hope certain people have learned from their mistakes and we won't have a repeat of last year's Christmas service." She looked sideways at Miriam Hodge.

"You know, Fern," I said, "some churches actually encourage their members to bring visitors to church. They've found it to be an effective way to share the gospel."

"Listen here, young man, when my grandmother staked out our pew in 1922, she did not intend for every Tom, Dick, or Harry to come along and plop his hiney down there."

"I must say I have to agree with Fern," Bea Majors said. "Elsewise, there'd be all types of rabble in here. They've already ruined our beautiful angels." She shuddered at the memory of it.

"Maybe we could run an advertisement in the *Herald* asking people not to come to our Christmas Eve worship," I suggested, trying not to sound ironic.

The elders pondered my counsel for several moments. "No, I don't think so," Fern said. "An ad would cost money. Why don't we just have Bea mention in the church column that nonmembers who attend our Christmas Eve service must bring their own cookies and chairs? That way it gets in the newspaper, but we don't have to pay for it."

"Good thinking," Bea said, writing a note to herself. "Consider it done."

"If you ask me," Dale Hinshaw said, "I think we oughta give serious thought to not even having our Christmas Eve service here in the meetinghouse. It's nothing but a mess. Kids bellyaching to ring the bell. Cookie crumbs everywhere. Toilets not getting flushed. Bulletins left on the pews. Took me and the missus two hours to get the place clean after last year's service. And we didn't even get to take us up an offering," he added, frowning in my direction.

The year before, I had recommended we not collect an offering at the Christmas Eve service. In the past, the pastor would pause in the reading of the Gospel of Luke so the ushers could collect an offering. The loot gathered, he would resume his reading and bring in the Christ child. It had always troubled me. "It looks like we're holding Christ hostage and won't let him loose until someone coughs up some money," I'd said. "I think we want to avoid sending that message."

"And just what are my ushers gonna do?" Dale asked. "It's our biggest collection of the year. Four ushers with two reserves and an extra counter. We've been practicin' for three months, and now you're telling us we're not welcome. How do you expect me to keep up their morale when you're stabbing 'em in the back like that."

Dale finally conceded when we agreed to have the ushers take up two offerings the following Sunday. But he'd been gunning for me ever since. Now he was suggesting we not hold our Christmas Eve service in our own meetinghouse.

"Dale, have you given any thought to where else we might hold our Christmas Eve service, if not here?" Miriam Hodge asked.

"Well, I've been thinkin' on that and I believe we oughta have ourselves a live Nativity scene."

Opal Majors groaned. "Not more livestock. When we had that Mohammed the Baptist here for our revival, I cleaned up after his camel a good month afterwards. I'd rather sweep up cookie crumbs."

"That's the beauty of it," Dale said. "We don't gotta have the Nativity scene here. We can have it at the park. We'll set it up in center field of the Little League diamond. That way folks'll have to get out of their cars and walk over to see it. By the time they get there, they'll be frozen stiff. Me and my ushers can set up a hot chocolate stand at first base and make a mint." He leaned back in his chair, a triumphant smile spreading across his face.

"I'm concerned how that will look," Miriam Hodge said. "Why don't we just give people hot chocolate? Why do we need to make money?"

"We wasn't gonna keep the money. I was thinkin' maybe we could give it to a good cause."

Opal Majors eyed him suspiciously. "You wouldn't be thinking of sending the money to that kook on the radio you've been listening to? That Eddie character who talks about the end times?"

"For your information, he's a recognized expert on the end times. And you'll be whistling a different tune when the Rapture comes and you're left to the devil for hinderin' the Lord's work."

I tried to get the meeting back on track. "Dale, I'm sure Eddie is sincere in his beliefs, and I'm glad you've found him helpful. But I'm not sure we can even hold a Nativity scene at a public park. It's probably against the law."

"Well, that's another thing Eddie warned about, how the end is near when you can't even talk about Jesus in a public place. I say we sue the town before it sues us. That'll teach 'em not to pick on the Lord."

I glanced at my watch. It was almost nine o'clock. If we ended the meeting now, I could be home in time to kiss my boys good night. "Why don't we pray about this matter, then discuss it further at our next meeting. It's only September, after all. We have plenty of time before Christmas." Then, before anyone could object, I bowed my head and closed in prayer.

The October meeting of the elders didn't fare any better. Dale accused Miriam Hodge of promoting one world order—yet another warning sign, according to Eddie, that the Rapture was near. Then Dale questioned the wisdom of having any Christmas Eve program. "The Lord'll probably be back by then, and we'd have wasted time planning for something that ain't even gonna happen. I say we just concern ourselves with gettin' as many folks as we can right with the Lord. Eddie thinks the Rapture could come any day now, maybe even next Tuesday."

Dale Hinshaw's membership on the board of elders has caused me to question God as nothing else ever has. How could an all-knowing, all-powerful, and all-loving God permit such a thing to happen, I asked my wife, after the October elders meeting.

"Maybe God isn't all-powerful," she suggested. "Maybe God shares power with us, so we can be a part of his work. Like Clarence the angel."

"Who's Clarence the angel?"

"You know, Clarence the angel in *It's a Wonderful Life*. He jumps off the bridge and saves Jimmy Stewart."

"Oh, that Clarence the angel. What's he got to do with anything?" I ask.

"I'm just saying that maybe God uses us like he used Clarence to help accomplish his purposes."

I pondered that for a moment. "There's only one problem with that theory," I said.

"What's that?"

"It would mean God had to depend on people like Dale Hinshaw."

She winced. "That is an alarming thought, isn't it?"

This is the problem of theology—instead of bringing clarity, it often raises questions too frightening to consider.

Some ministers' wives memorize Scripture; my wife finds solace in old movies. *It's a Wonderful Life* is her favorite. Our town doesn't have cable television, but Clevis Nagle, the owner of the Royal Theater, shows *It's a Wonderful Life* for free just before Christmas. When I was growing up, I would attend with my parents and brother, Roger. We'd buy our popcorn, then take our place in the fifth row from the back, left side. Everyone else knew better than to sit there.

By craning my neck, I could peer through the gap in the curtain and watch Nora Nagle, the future state Sausage Queen, working the popcorn machine. For a number of years, the smell of popcorn had a carnal effect on me. One whiff of popcorn and I had thoughts true Christians shouldn't have. At least if you took Matthew 5:28 literally, which, growing up where I did, was the only way to take it.

As a teenager, obsessed with piety, I considered either plucking out my eyes (per Matthew 5:29) or cutting off my nose, thereby eliminating my olfactory capacity and, with it, the temptation to sin. I did neither, opting instead to wear nose plugs to the Royal Theater. While this had a chilling effect on my reputation, it kept me blameless against the day Jesus would return to take my soul to heaven.

Still, I had dreams of Jesus coming back and finding me in the movie theater.

"But I was wearing nose plugs," I would plead with Jesus.

"That might be, but you were still watching Nora Nagle through the gap in the curtain," He would say, leaving my sorry carcass behind for the dogs to chew on.

In time, these worries passed, for which I'm grateful, as fear of the Divine is a heavy burden. Which is why I feel sorry for Dale Hinshaw, who goes through life with a wary eye cast toward the heavens. He listens to Eddie talk on the radio about the unforgivable sin—grieving the Holy Spirit. Dale worries he might have accidentally done that, and thinks extra zeal on his part might get him off the hook. This is why he keeps nominating himself to serve as an elder. He hopes God will think twice before smiting a leader of the church.

Dale took it upon himself to stop by Owen Stout's law office to inquire if the church could hold a Nativity scene on public property. Owen didn't think so. "'Fraid not, Dale. All we'd need is for the ACLU to find out and sue the skivvies right off of you and all the other elders. You could maybe even lose your homes."

This did not deter Dale from encouraging the other elders to stand strong for the Lord at our November meeting. "Let 'em have our houses, I don't care. I'd rather be homeless and show the world I loved the Lord than live in a fancy mansion and be afraid to call myself a Christian. How many of you are willin' to stand up for the Lord, even it means losin' your house? Raise your hands."

"But I like my house," Bea Majors said. "Besides, I just got new carpet for my living room."

"Is there any way we can love the Lord and still keep our homes?" Asa Peacock asked. "My house has been in my family since 1893. I'd kinda hate to lose it. If I'd known that was gonna happen, I'd have never agreed to be an elder. Sam, you didn't tell me about this. You just said there'd be one meeting a month, and that I wouldn't have to pray in public unless I wanted to. You didn't say nothing about me having to give up my house."

It took me half an hour to settle Dale down and convince the elders they could keep their homes. I finally told them we could have the live Nativity scene in my yard.

"Oh, sure," Dale groused. "Hog all the glory for yourself. Why can't we have it at my house?"

"That's fine with me, Dale. I just thought it would help matters along if I volunteered my yard, that's all."

"How come Dale always gets his way?" Bea Majors complained. "Why couldn't we have it at my house? I might not have a big, fancy house like certain other people, but it's not a dump either."

"I'm sure Jessie wouldn't mind if we had the Nativity scene in our yard," Asa Peacock volunteered. "She was saying just the other day that she wanted to do more with the church."

Fern Hampton let out a heavy sigh. "I've been a member of this church all my life and we've never had one thing at my house. Not one thing. It's like the rest of you don't even want to be around me."

"Why don't we find a way to share?" Miriam Hodge suggested. "That way everyone can be involved."

Yes, sharing was a grand idea. We appointed Dale Hinshaw to work out the details and proceed. By then it was ten o'clock, and I was wrung out. Christmas was five weeks away, and I was already exhausted. Walking home, I had a creeping dread about how a Nativity scene could be shared. But I shrugged it off, and thought how glad I would be when Christ got here, so life could get back to normal.

Surprisingly, the next few weeks were blissful. Dale made himself scarce, though rumors circulated of his whereabouts: he was seen at the lumberyard buying wood for a manger, he'd stopped by Ellis Hodge's farm to borrow assorted livestock, he and the missus were seen buying material and a bathrobe pattern at Kivett's Five and Dime. In real fact, it was the calm before the Christmas storm.

four

Preparations

Barbara and I took the boys to see Santa Claus at Kivett's Five and Dime. Bud Matthews is in the nursing home these days with bats in his attic. He thinks it's 1943 and the Germans are after him. He props a chair in front of his door and only lets someone in if they can tell him who the starting pitcher for the Yankees in the third game of the 1939 World Series was. The nurses have written *Lefty Gomez* on a piece of paper and taped it to the outside of his door.

With Bud off to the front, his son Ernie has assumed his Santa legacy and holds forth each Saturday in December. He doesn't have his father's flair for the role. His pants hang low, exposing his backside. He takes a fifteen-minute break every two hours when he smokes a cigarette out front of the store, in plain view of the children. We're accustomed to it, but people new to town complain to Ned Kivett about him. Ned smiles, nods his head, and agrees to look into the matter. It takes about three years for the people who move here to realize that when we smile, nod, and agree to look into a certain matter, it means we're just being polite and have no intention of changing.

The philosopher Blaise Pascal reasoned that if God is real, then believing in Him would be profitable. If God doesn't exist, no harm is done in believing, so the prudent person believes. This is our son Levi's philosophy about Santa. Better to go along with it than risk waking up to an empty tree. He sits on Santa's lap, pulls a list from his pocket, and proceeds to ask for the very things we've forbidden him—his own television set, a BB gun, a dirt bike, and various reptiles.

Our son Addison draws near to Santa, his hands clasped, his eyes wide with awe. He is like a pilgrim approaching Jerusalem. When Ernie asks him what he wants, he babbles incoherently as if speaking in tongues. Ernie has to guess. "How about a truck? Ya wanna truck?" He already has a dozen trucks, but his ability to reason has failed. He nods his head. "Yes. Truck."

Then Ned Kivett's wife, Racine, takes their picture for three dollars, which is used to buy presents for the poor children in town. She and Ned distribute the gifts the week before Christmas. The poor do not apply for assistance. It's a small town; we know who they are. Or think we do. If you see Ned and Racine coming up your sidewalk the week before Christmas, you've either had a hard year, or people have been talking about you behind your back.

In addition to the poor children, they give presents to the kids who are sick. But they have to be real sick. A head cold won't do. It has to be leprosy or the plague or something like that. When I was growing up, Uly Grant had a knack for contracting odd diseases the week before Christmas and raking it in.

Kivett's Five and Dime is the only game in town, Christmas-wise. People are too suspicious to order from catalogs, thanks to stories Ned has told over the years about catalog merchants buying cocaine and supporting leftist governments with the very money God-fearing Americans have sent them. "You buy underwear from me, and you know where the money's going," he tells his customers. "Right back in your pockets, in your businesses, helping you." He has a sign in his window that reads, *Be Harmonian. Buy Harmonian.*

For a number of years, he had a gift-buying service for the men in town. For five extra dollars, Racine would select an appropriate gift, wrap it, and deliver it to the doorstep of your beloved the day before Christmas. One year, she delivered Pastor Taylor's wife a size-six negligee with a name tag that read, *To my lovely Samantha.* Everyone who saw it agreed it was a beautiful garment. The only problem was that Pastor Taylor's wife was named Erma and she hadn't seen size six for a good decade. That year we had store-bought cookies at the Christmas Eve service. Ned ended the gift-buying service shortly thereafter.

Now we men have to pick out our own gifts. Ned sets up a table of suitable gifts for us to peruse—waffle irons, dishware, towel sets, salt-and-pepper shakers in the shape of various fowl, corn-on-the-cob holders. Racine wraps our presents for an extra dollar. She peers at our selections. "Are you sure you want to go with these oven mitts?" she asks. "How about a necklace? We have some lovely necklaces."

No, we tell her, not for our wives, who are sensible women and would be upset if we wasted our money on such frivolities. Besides, they loved the oven mitts we bought last year. Racine sighs, puts the oven mitts in a box, and wraps them in gold paper, marveling that the divorce rate in our town isn't any higher than it is. But we know our wives. We tried necklaces and flowers and other fineries, only to be scolded for our extravagance. We were told we shouldn't have, that it cost too much, that the neighbors would think we were showing off. After a few years we believed them and went with oven mitts and corn-on-the-cob holders.

I bought my wife a new toaster. I worried when I bought it that it might be too lavish a gift. It was a four-slotter with a knife sharpener, plus the slots adjusted to toast bagels. I debated for an hour whether to buy it. I imagined having to spend Christmas listening to her say that I really shouldn't have, that it cost too much, that the two-slotter would have been perfectly fine.

Racine mentioned my wife had been in the day before looking at the bracelets. "We have some very nice ones. I can show you the one she was looking at, if you'd like."

I explained to Racine that my wife has a rare skin condition and can't wear jewelry. "The first year we were married, I bought her a bracelet and it turned her wrist green."

Racine sighs and wraps the toaster.

My sons are with me. I give them ten dollars to buy their mommy a gift. They pore over Ned's table, finally settling on an assortment of pot scrubbers and a ceramic frog pot-scrubber holder. Racine suggests a silver picture frame to hold a picture of the boys. Levi and Addison don't think so. "She spends a lot more time washing dishes than she does looking at pictures," Levi points out. I look down at my sons and beam with pride. That they have mastered the subtleties of gift giving at such a tender age thrills me. Racine sighs and wraps the pot scrubbers.

With our gift buying accomplished, we head over to the Coffee Cup for lunch—hamburgers, french fries, and, since their mother isn't there, Coke instead of milk. They drown their fries with catsup. They would chug it straight from the bottle if I let them. Penny has two pieces of chocolate cake left over from the day before, which she gives to the boys. Coke, catsup, and cake, the trinity of little-boy food. By the time I settle the bill with Vinny, they are running wide open, their gas pedals pressed to the floor.

We collect our presents and go past Grant's Hardware to look at the Christmas trees. I am descended from a long line of Christmas tree connoisseurs. The boys and I poke around, looking for the Holy Grail of trees. We bend the needles to check for freshness. We inspect the trunks for what my father calls "vertical integrity." The ceiling in our living room is ten feet high. Our angel is thirteen inches. I like to give her a little haloroom, so we look for an eight-foot tree.

Spruce trees are the best, but also the most expensive. When I tell my wife how much they cost, she suggests an artificial tree would pay for itself in two years. Not only that, she says, it would be safer. She recalls horrific stories about Christmas trees spontaneously combusting and burning down entire city blocks.

I try to shield my boys from such heresy. Being young and unformed, they are vulnerable to deception. I let them wander amongst the trees, inhaling the balsam. Artificial trees, I tell them, emit toxic chemicals known to cause birth defects in rats. Sure, they're cheaper, I admit, but when your child is born with an arm growing out of his forehead, will the money you saved be a comfort? I encourage them to take the long view.

We find the perfect tree—the needles bend without breaking, good vertical integrity, an inch shy of eight feet. Uly Grant and I carry it to his pickup truck. The boys and I arrange ourselves in the back for the ride home. Left on Marion Street, a right at the library, down three blocks, through the alley, and we're home.

When we'd bought the house from Dr. Neely, he'd advised us to put the tree in front of the window across from the fireplace. There was a small hook protruding from the window sill. "The floor tilts a bit, so just run some fishing line from the hook to the top of the tree and you'll be fine." So that's what we do.

We wrestled the tree through the door, arranged it in the stand, screwed the bolts down tight against the tree, then ran the fishing line and pulled the tree upright. Next came the lights, then the ornaments, the icicles, and the angel. The boys pawed through the box looking for the Christmas elf, which my mother gave me when I was seven years old. They hide him in the branches near the trunk, this tiny elf, wearing a red hat and tunic, with a matching red face from when he sat next to a Christmas bulb in 1974 and was permanently sunburned. It is unsettling to think such a calamity could have happened under the watchful gaze of an angel, but such is the mystery of suffering.

Despite her pro–artificial tree sentiments, my wife admires the tree. She inhales deeply, then smiles. "It does smell nice," she concedes. "Just be sure to keep it watered. I don't want it exploding."

The next day we stayed after worship and set up a tree in the meetinghouse. When I was a child, Dale Hinshaw heard a radio preacher allege that Christmas trees had their origins in an ancient cult that worshiped evergreens. Dale didn't see how he could remain a member of a church that had cast its lot with Satan, so he left. He stayed away for three weeks, certain we would beg him to return. When we didn't, he came back anyway, convinced we were so desperately lost he needed to stick around and lead us into Truth.

These days, his prophecy takes the form of an annual exhortation for us to reject Christmas trees and return to righteousness, lest the Lord's anger be kindled against us. "We're all the time hearing about these Christmas trees catching fire. Did you ever think that might be the Lord's way of warning us?"

People are in no mood to listen this year. They're upset with Dale for replacing the Christmas Eve program with a live Nativity scene. It wasn't all Dale's doing, but the other elders won't shoulder the blame. They nod in agreement, then pin it on Dale. This is the chief convenience of having him in our fellowship. Though a boil on our backside, he is also a convenient scapegoat. Being irritated at Dale is our common bond; our shared exasperation is the tie that binds.

"I've been getting a lot of phone calls about not having the Christmas Eve service," Frank, my secretary, told me. "Folks are awful mad. What do you want me to tell 'em?"

"Have them call Dale," I said. "He's in charge of this year's Christmas program."

"What's he got planned?"

"Some kind of Nativity scene. The last I heard he'd borrowed three pigs and a cow from Ellis Hodge. Personally, I'm staying out of it. I want deniability in case it flops."

"Smart thinking, Sam."

Dale stopped by the office later that day. He was worked into a lather. "I was laying carpet in the manger and Bernie pulled up in his police car and told me I needed a building permit. Can you believe that? Here I am doin' the Lord's work, and he's writin' me out a citation."

"You were carpeting the manger?"

"Yep. Bea Majors had some left over from her living room."

"I wasn't aware they had carpet back then."

"Well sure they did. What'd you think they used? Linoleum? Boy, for someone who's been to college, you sure don't know your history."

He flopped himself down in the chair across from my desk. "The building permit's the bad news," he said. "The good news is that we got the materials for the manger for free from Uly Grant. All we gotta do is paint *Compliments of Grant's Hardware* on the side of the manger."

This is what came from putting Dale Hinshaw in charge. The birth of Jesus was now compliments of Grant's Hardware.

"Are you sure we want to paint that on the manger, Dale?"

"Got to," he said. "The sign thanking Asa Peacock for donating the straw is gonna be in front. I don't want two signs out front—it'd block the view of the radio man."

"Radio man?"

"You betcha." He smiled proudly. "I called WEAK over in Cartersburg, and they're sending a fella over to do a live broadcast from the manger."

"Won't that seem out of place?"

43

"Nah, he's gonna wear a bathrobe and be a fourth wise man."

"Four wise men. I see. That sounds a little crowded."

He frowned. "Yeah, it is getting a little full. I'll have to think on that some." He rose up from the chair. "Well, I gotta get going. Bob Miles wants to interview me about the Nativity scene for the *Herald*." He paused in the doorway. "Say, you wouldn't know anybody who's got a baby, would you? We need a Baby Jesus."

"Why don't you see if Kivett's will donate a toy doll," I suggested. "They look pretty close to the real thing."

As soon as I said it, I regretted it. I had a vision of Dale painting *This Year's Messiah Compliments of Kivett's Five and Dime* on the other side of the manger.

When Dale left, Frank the secretary leaned in the doorway of my office. "Did I hear you say something about Kivett's?"

"Yeah, Dale's gonna ask Ned to donate a doll for the Baby Jesus."

Frank looked wistful. "Remember when Bud Matthews was Santa? Martha and I'd take Susan down there when she was a little girl. Oh, she used to love that. Boy, what I wouldn't give to have those days back."

Frank's wife, Martha, had died several years before, and Susan, their only child, lived in North Carolina. Frank had told me she wouldn't be coming home for the holidays.

"What are you doing for Christmas?" I asked. "Wanna come to our house? We'd love to have you."

"No, that's okay. I'll be fine. Thanks just the same. I was thinking I'd go sit with Bud Matthews at the nursing home."

"Don't forget to yell out 'Lefty Gomez' so he'll let you in his room," I reminded him.

Frank chuckled. "I remember that game. Third game of the '39 World Series. I listened to it with my dad. We carried the radio out to the front porch and heard the whole game."

He grew quiet, remembering.

You close your eyes in a dead-still room and rewind the tape. Revisit snatches of time. A late summer day with your father on the porch. You are eight years old, he is your world. Spin forward. Taking your daughter by her hand, setting her on Santa's lap. Sorting through the Christmas trees, searching for perfection. Coming home after midnight from the Christmas Eve service, carrying your little girl up the stairs, tucking her in, then staying up to set presents under the tree.

Frank always thought his wife would be around to recollect such things, that these soft memories would be a bulwark against hard times. But it doesn't work that way. He tries to keep busy, thinking busyness will be a sturdy brace against the heavy weight of time and sorrow. He makes his rounds, visiting the loners. But the people present don't always make up for the people gone. He used to think having the memories almost made up for not having the person, but now he's not so sure.

The Unveiling

*T*wo weeks before Christmas, my office phone rang. It was Miriam Hodge, informing me that a special meeting of the elders committee had been called. There went my dream of a meeting-free month.

"I thought we were going to take December off," I said.

Miriam sighed. "Dale Hinshaw asked to have a meeting, and got Opal Majors to go along. According to the rules, if two elders ask for a meeting, we have to do it."

"What's he want to talk about?"

"He mentioned something about running the plans for the Nativity scene by us."

"For crying out loud," I said. "How hard can it be? You nail together some boards, get a few people to stand around

47

in bathrobes, throw a cow or two in the mix and you're halfway home. What's the big deal?"

"I'm not sure, but he wants to meet tonight at seven."

"Tonight! Tonight's the night Clevis Nagle is showing *It's a Wonderful Life* at the Royal. I promised my wife and boys I'd take them. Rats!"

"Sam, why don't you go ahead and take them. I'll go to the meeting, then call you tomorrow to tell you what he's up to. Sound good?"

"Thank you, Miriam. That's real sweet of you. I appreciate your kindness."

Having wormed my way out of an evening with Dale Hinshaw, I was in a mood to celebrate and offered to treat Frank to lunch at the Coffee Cup. We walked down the street, pulled open the door, and the bell tinkled as we went in. Vinny Toricelli looked up from the grill. "Change the subject, boys," he called out. "The preacher's here."

There's a price to be paid for pastoring in a small town. I never hear the juicier gossip, and the jokes are limited to priest-minister-and-rabbi golfing jokes, which I've heard a million times but have to laugh at anyway, lest I appear to be a poor sport.

Frank and I found a corner booth, across the room from the buffet, away from the traffic. I had to endure a few minutes of good-natured insults before the diners turned on someone else and I could study the menu in peace. Friday is meat-loaf day, unless you're Catholic; then Vinny has codfish with tartar sauce, your choice of two sides, and sweet iced tea. With sufficient catsup, the meat loaf is tolerable, so I ordered that. Frank had the codfish, in honor of his deceased Catholic grandmother, who'd married a Protestant and was disowned by her family.

Frank makes it a point to mention that he is one-fourth Catholic whenever Dale is around. Dale pleads with him to listen to Eddie on the radio and learn the real truth about Catholics, the stuff the pope doesn't want you to know. Like how if a Protestant marries a Catholic and they divorce, the Catholic gets the kids because of a secret deal the pope made with President Kennedy. If the Catholic parent dies, the pope gets the kids, which is why the pope's house is so big. It is full of half-Protestant children who are being brainwashed. Eddie has discovered secret documents bearing this out, and he's written a book, which Dale bought and gave to Frank, to no avail.

The bell over the door tinkled. I saw Frank grimace, so I turned and looked. It was Dale. He slid into the booth next to me just as Penny brought our food. Frank bowed his head to pray. It was unusual for Frank to take the initiative in prayer, but Dale and I bowed our heads with him. "Bless us, O Lord, and these thy gifts, which we are about to receive through thy bounty, through Christ, our Lord, Amen." Then Frank crossed himself, raised his head, spread his napkin across his lap, and began eating his codfish.

Dale peered at him. "What kind of prayer was that?" he asked. "I never heard that one."

"It's Catholic," Frank said. "My grandmother taught it to me. And since you bowed your head and prayed it with me, that makes you a Catholic now."

Well, Eddie had warned about things like this on the radio, but Dale couldn't believe he'd been tricked into joining the Roman Catholic Church. He was livid. He jumped up from the booth and stalked out of the Coffee Cup, fuming.

"That's one way to get rid of him, I suppose," Frank said, laughing.

"You should be ashamed of yourself, treating him like that," I said, trying to look stern, but not having much luck. "We'll pay for that, you know."

"Yeah, probably," he admitted. "But I couldn't resist."

With Dale gone, it was a pleasant meal. At noon, the siren at the fire station sounded. We checked our watches, then Vinny flipped on the television to watch the news from the city. All over the restaurant, men set down their forks to watch the mayhem. The general consensus was the same as always—that we are fortunate to live in this town where the only wacko is Dale Hinshaw, who is annoying, but relatively harmless.

I finished my sermon that afternoon, went home, ate supper, then walked the three blocks to the Royal with my family to watch *It's a Wonderful Life.* Clevis Nagle was there in his black pants, white shirt, and red bow tie. His daughter Nora was manning the concession stand. She is back home after a twenty-year sojourn in California, where she almost hit it big as a dancing grape in an underwear commercial.

People have been talking about her, how her success in life came too early, before she was prepared. First, being crowned Sausage Queen at our Corn and Sausage Days festival, winning the state Sausage Queen contest, then moving to Hollywood and starring in an underwear commercial. It was too much too quick. Now she's forty and washed up, her glory years but a memory. At least that's the talk around town. She's back to serving popcorn at the Royal on Friday nights and working weekdays as a checkout girl at Kivett's Five and Dime. But she doesn't look washed up to me, and it's hard not to watch her through the gap in the curtain, as I did when I was a teenager.

I didn't follow the movie closely. I've seen it thirty-five times, every year since I was six and Clevis began showing it for free. Instead, I thought about the elders over at the meetinghouse and wondered what they were doing. I hoped Miriam was able to rein Dale in, but had my doubts. He was probably up to six signs and five wise men by now.

I dozed for a while, then came to just as Clarence the angel showed up to save Jimmy Stewart. I wished Clarence went to our church. Maybe he could work on Dale. I leaned over to my wife. "Is Clarence still alive?"

She shook her head no. "Died in 1965. Arteriosclerosis."

So much for that idea.

I scrunched down in the seat when it got to where everyone is giving Jimmy Stewart money. I always cry at that part and didn't want people to see me. I sat in my chair wishing Clarence were still alive. Arteriosclerosis. I'd had no idea, or I'd have sent a card. I felt terrible. A tear slid down my cheek.

Then the bell on the tree rang, Jimmy Stewart winked at Clarence, and the movie was over. Clevis Nagle turned on the house lights. We stood and stretched while our pupils shrank. My wife looked at me. "Why are your eyes red?"

"It must be the horsehair in these old seats," I said. "I think I'm allergic to it."

We walked past the popcorn machine. Nora Nagle glanced at me. I'm a happily married man, so I tried not to think of her riding in Ellis Hodge's hay wagon in her dressing gown twenty-five years before. I wondered if Dale might ask her to reprise her role as Mary for this year's

Nativity. For the first time in history, wives wouldn't have to plead with their husbands to come to a church activity. They'd show up in droves, in their funeral suits and doused in Old Spice, their hair combed over in wings, just to gaze upon the heavenly vision that was Nora Nagle.

She smiled at me. Her gaze lingered. Maybe it was my imagination, but she seemed to regret that I was married. She appeared to be saying something. She arched her eyebrows. Her lips moved. Now she was staring directly at me, as if we were the only two in the theater. She wanted to speak of regrets and love unclaimed, I could tell. I heard a voice. "Daddy, I have to go pee-pee. Can you take me?" Nora Nagle turned back to the popcorn machine, the spell broken.

It reminded me why it had been twenty-five years since we'd had a Nativity scene. It presented too great a temptation—a virgin in a bathrobe. Unless we asked Fern Hampton to play the Virgin Mary. That would stifle all thoughts of carnality.

It snowed that night, so the next morning I took my boys sledding on the hill at the park. That afternoon, the phone rang. It was Miriam Hodge. I asked her how the elders meeting went.

"Not well," she said. "Not well at all."

"What happened?"

"Dale wants to have a progressive Nativity scene."

"A what?" I asked.

"A progressive Nativity scene," she repeated.

I'd heard of progressive dinners, but never of a progressive Nativity scene. "What in the world is that?"

"He wouldn't say. He said he wanted everyone to hear it at the same time. He's going to talk about it during the announcement time at church tomorrow."

This was a favorite ploy of Dale Hinshaw—to trap us in the meeting room, rise to his feet, and rattle on about all sorts of matters.

I tried to put it out of my mind, but the prospect of Dale Hinshaw hijacking worship chilled my enthusiasm for Christian community. I went to bed early that night, but couldn't sleep for thinking about Dale and what he might do. Downstairs, I could hear the clock strike two. I sighed. Barbara rolled over to me. "Having trouble sleeping?" she asked.

"Yeah. Sorry. Didn't aim to keep you up."

"Oh, that's okay. What are you thinking about?"

"Dale, of course. You know, I spent twenty hours this week working on my sermon, and now people won't even be in the mood to hear it. Dale'll stand and babble for twenty minutes and people will be worn out before it's even time for the sermon."

"Well, the good thing is, if they don't pay attention to

your sermon tomorrow, you can always preach it again next Sunday and they'll never notice."

I chuckled.

"Whose idea was it to put Dale Hinshaw in charge of the Christmas program anyway?" she asked.

I didn't say anything for a moment. It didn't take her long to figure out. "I thought it would help him feel included," I explained.

I could feel her stare in the dark. "Why didn't you just invite him out for coffee?"

Why, indeed.

Sunday morning dawned bright and cold. I skipped Sunday school in order to preserve my strength for worship. Sunday school was a discouragement to me. Nineteen adults sitting around two tables in the basement while Bea Majors read aloud from *The Sword of the Lord* magazine was not my idea of Christian education.

I had given serious thought to skipping the announcements, but realized that wouldn't help. Dale would stand anyway, probably at the most inopportune moment, during the middle of my sermon for instance, and begin distributing mimeographed handouts of his latest scheme. I decided to get it over with.

My usual practice was to first read the announcements in the bulletin, the necessity of which mystified me. These were literate people; they knew how to read. But reading the bulletin aloud was a cherished tradition, so I was stuck with the task. Then I would ask if anyone had any additional announcements. This morning, I skipped right to that part. Dale hesitated. My going out of order had thrown him off. He glanced around, then rose to his feet. "Uh, there's something I need to announce."

I could hear faint sighs around the meetinghouse.

In an effort to appear pastoral, I smiled at Dale. "Yes, Dale?"

"Well, I just want to encourage everyone to attend our first annual progressive Nativity scene." The first annual progressive Nativity scene! Now we were doomed to repeat it, year after year, until Dale died.

"When I started workin' on this," Dale said, "I didn't realize just how big your average Nativity scene was. You got your manger and your Holy Family and your shepherds and angels and wise men, not to mention your cows and pigs and geese. Then there's all the signs for your corporate sponsors, and your concession stand. Then on top of that, you got the angel of the Lord and the spotlights and the sound system. Well, there just ain't no one place big enough. So I set to praying on it, and the Lord told me what to do. He said, 'Dale, I want you to spread out the Nativity scene all over town.' So that's what we're gonna do. We'll start with the manger in my yard and put the livestock in Sam's yard. The Holy Family can go in Asa and Jessie's yard, and the wise men, they can go in Bea's yard. Now Fern said she'd be happy to put the shepherds at her place. And here's the good part. We can draw us up a map and give it to folks for a ten-dollar donation, like them ministers do on TV, and folks can drive past the various scenes in the order they appear in Scripture."

To say we were stunned was an understatement.

I glanced over at Miriam Hodge. Ordinarily unflappable, she sat with her eyes rolled back in her head. Her husband, Ellis, was fanning her with a "Jesus at the Last Supper" cardboard fan, compliments of the Johnny Mackey Funeral Parlor.

This image would stay indelibly fixed in my mind—Dale Hinshaw smiling triumphantly while the congregation looked on in various degrees of shock and dismay. I glanced at my wife. She had rocked back in her pew, not exactly charmed with the idea of livestock foraging in our front yard.

But Dale wasn't finished. "Uh, I'm gonna need the ushers to meet at Asa Peacock's farm this Tuesday for target practice, just in case some wacko terrorist tries infiltratin' our progressive Nativity scene." And with that, he sat down.

It is a sad fact that the topics a pastor studies in seminary seldom cover the exigencies of real life. There is no class on

Dale Hinshaw. Lacking such knowledge, I descended to my baser self and did something of which I am ashamed to this day. I bowed my head and prayed that God, in His tender mercy, might strike Dale down. Nothing fatal, I specified to the Lord, just something sufficiently miserable to confine him to bed. Maybe temporary paralysis from a spider bite, or a two-week coma followed by a miraculous recovery.

"And quickly, Lord," I added. "Before word gets out."

On the Verge

I have long marveled at the correlation between time and misery. The more I dread the arrival of a loathsome event, the quicker that occasion seems to arrive. The week had flown past since Dale's unveiling of his progressive Nativity scene. Despite my prayers, he remained in excellent health, and word of our progressive Nativity scene had spread all over town. My fellow pastors had phoned to commiserate. A few, I could tell, were trying hard not to laugh.

Bob Miles from the *Harmony Herald* called to say his wife's first cousin was next-door neighbors with a janitor at the city newspaper. "If you want," he suggested, "maybe I can pull a few strings and get a reporter down here to do a write-up on this Nativity program of yours."

Now it was my Nativity program.

I thanked him for his kindness, but told him we wanted to keep it low-key for the sake of dignity. But in that week's edition of the *Herald,* Bea Majors devoted her entire church column to the progressive Nativity scene.

Harmony Friends Meeting
by Bea Majors

We will not be holding our regular Christmas Eve service because it is too much bother. Please join us for our First Annual Progressive Nativity Scene beginning at Dale Hinshaw's house at 7 P.M. The event is free, but the purchase of a map is required; the map can be purchased at the church for $10. Hot chocolate and cookies will be sold at the Fern Hampton residence. The Progressive Nativity Scene will be simulcast on WEAK (AM 1230). Additional volunteers are needed for security. Interested persons may phone Dale Hinshaw. Experience with firearms preferred.

Fern Hampton had persuaded the Friendly Women's Circle to sell the cookies and hot chocolate in order to raise money for Brother Norman's shoe ministry to the Choctaw Indians. Ordinarily, their fund-raiser for the Choctaws was the annual Chicken Noodle Dinner held during Corn and

Sausage Days. But this year, the Circle had used that money to buy a vanity for the women's rest room.

In mid-December, Brother Norman had mailed the Circle a Christmas letter in which he'd expressed his happiness that the Lord had blessed the good ladies of the Circle, then asked their prayers for numerous Choctaw children who'd stepped on rusty nails and nearly died of tetanus. It was due to a shoe shortage, Brother Norman explained, because certain donations they had been counting on had not come through. He hoped it wouldn't lead to amputations, but he couldn't be sure. He asked them to be in prayer, but only if they had the time. He didn't want to inconvenience them.

Fern felt terrible. She tossed and turned all that night, tormented by the thought of shoeless Choctaw children hobbling around. When she woke up and opened her closet to get her slippers, there were her shoes, lined up in neat rows. She counted six pairs. "Lord, forgive me," she prayed. "I'm the Imelda Marcos of Harmony."

She began working the phones, summoning the Friendly Women to action. She divided the women into two committees, the hot chocolate committee and the cookie committee. She drafted Ellis Hodge to haul three tables over from the church basement and set them up in her garage. Then, to ease her guilt, she went to the Kroger and bought two hundred Styrofoam hot-chocolate cups with her own money.

Fern had been feeling dispirited, but this noble cause revived her and gave her purpose. She cleaned the garage and took a load of junk to the dump, where she rooted around for shoes for the Choctaw children. She found five perfectly good pairs. She shook her head at the waste. She thought of her father, who had grown up so poor he had to share a pair of shoes with his brother. "He wore the left shoe, and I got the right one," he'd told her. "We had to hop to school."

People these days don't know what it's like to go without, Fern thought to herself. Maybe that Eddie guy on the radio who Dale listened to was right. Maybe these were the last days, with all their greed and filth and violence. People laughed at Dale, but maybe he had a point. They wouldn't be laughing when some wacko terrorist took over the progressive Nativity scene. She made a note to herself to ask Dale for extra security at the hot-chocolate stand.

People have been upset with Bea Majors for her newspaper column. Miriam Hodge complained about it at the meeting of the hot-chocolate committee. "Experience with firearms preferred! I can't believe she wrote that. It makes us look like crackpots."

That was Miriam for you, Fern thought. She liked Miriam, but believed she was a bit naïve, that she got a little carried away with this love-your-neighbor stuff. She'd given Miriam something to mull over. "You know, Miriam, what would happen if everyone thought like you? We'd all be speaking Chinese, that's what."

Bea began writing the church column back in 1971, at the request of Bob Miles's father, who had run the *Herald* in those days. Bea hadn't asked the elders or anything. She just started writing the column, along with her editorial comments. If the church was sponsoring an event she didn't approve of, she wouldn't mention it. Or worse, she'd mangle the announcement on purpose.

Like the time I'd invited my professor from seminary to speak at church and Bea had misquoted the date so people wouldn't show up. Bea thought he was a menace, because he'd written a book questioning the Virgin Birth and suggesting that some of the red verses in the Bible might not have actually been said by Jesus.

"It's right there in red ink," she'd said. "How can he deny it? It's as plain as the nose on your face."

She'd changed the date in her church column to confuse the liberals, who'd shown up that Sunday to have their sin glossed over, but instead heard a rousing presentation from the Friendly Women on the wide path that leads to death.

It was difficult to work up enthusiasm for Christmas in my present surroundings. Between Bea's newspaper column and Dale's formation of a Quaker militia, my Yuletide passion had withered considerably. I still had three days of vacation left. I kicked around the idea of taking Christmas Eve off and visiting my in-laws a hundred miles away. But the last time I'd done that, Dale had taken advantage of my absence by inviting Billy Bundle, the World's Shortest Evangelist, to speak at church. I'd simply be trading one mess for another.

The Tuesday before Christmas, I was seated at my office desk working on my sermon, when the phone rang. Frank picked it up. After a short pause, he yelled back that it was my wife. "She doesn't sound too happy, either," he added.

I picked up the phone. "Hi, honey. Is everything all right?"

At first, I couldn't understand what she was saying. I could only make sense of an occasional word here and there. "Pigs everywhere . . . Dale . . . tearing up the yard . . . geese . . . cows . . . Come home now! "

It was three days till Christmas. If I started driving now, I could be in Mexico before Christmas Eve. They'd never find me there. I could change my name and hide out in a monastery. But the obligation of family weighs heavily, so I went home instead to face whatever problem Dale had left in his wake.

He was still there when I arrived, stowing the ramp on Ellis Hodge's livestock truck. My wife was in our front yard nudging a pig out of her flower bed. A goose came my direction with a purposeful waddle, looking considerably agitated.

"Grab that goose, would ya?" Dale yelled.

I wasn't sure how to grab a goose, so I stepped aside and let him pass.

"What's going on here, Dale? What are all these animals doing here?"

"Today's the only day I could get Ellis's truck, so here I am."

"What am I supposed to do with these animals, Dale?"

"Oh, just keep 'em fed and watered. I'll be back to get 'em on the twenty-eighth, just as soon as we get home. We're leavin' for the sister-in-law's house on Christmas afternoon, but we'll be back on the twenty-eighth, the thirtieth at the latest."

He pulled a piece of paper from his back pocket and studied it. "Well, gotta go, Sam. Gotta get the manger set up. Then I'm off to target practice. We're practicin' our night ops tonight. I tell you, Sam, I never knew having a Nativity scene was such work." He shook his head at the complexity of it, then climbed in the truck. "Oh, yeah, I almost forgot. Ellis said to be sure and save the manure. He wants it for his garden. Just put it in your garage and he'll be by for it later." And with that, he wrestled the truck into first gear, moved forward with a lurch, and drove down the street.

I turned toward my wife and offered her a weak smile. "Hi, honey. So how's your day been?"

"Sam Gardner, if you think I'm going to have these animals in my yard, you have another think coming. I want them out, and I want them out now!"

"Well now, honey, it's only for a few days, and I bet we'll hardly notice them after a while."

I managed to corral the livestock in the garage before supper, but as we sat down to eat, the telephone rang. It was Uly Grant from the hardware store.

"Say, we got a goose down here, and someone thought it might be yours."

"Could you describe it, please?"

"Uh, sure. It's white and has kind of an orangish beak, and it looks mad. It's hissing a lot and stamping its feet."

"Yep, that sounds like one of mine," I said. "I'll be right over."

Fortunately, Uly had duct-taped its beak to keep it from biting anyone, though it still managed to clobber me in the head with its wings before I could wrestle it into the trunk of my car.

"So is it a pet, or what?" Uly asked.

"No, it belongs to Ellis Hodge. We're using it for our progressive Nativity scene at church. The animals are at my house."

I drove the goose home past Dale's house. Dale was up in a tree, stringing wire to a floodlight. The manger was erected on his front lawn. I could glimpse blue shag carpet covering the manger floor. Ten feet above the manger, tied in a tree, was a mannequin I recognized from Kivett's Five and Dime, garbed in a flannel shirt and blue jeans. I pulled over for a closer look. Dale climbed down from the tree.

"What's Ned Kivett's mannequin doing up in the tree?" I asked.

"That's the angel of the Lord," he explained.

"Oh, I see. I always thought angels of the Lord had wings and wore white robes."

"Yeah, well, Ned said I could borrow the mannequin so long as I didn't change its clothes."

I peered closer at the angel of the Lord. There was a sign I hadn't noticed at first, tied to a branch beside the angel. *All Flannel Shirts Now 10% Off During the Christmas Season.*

"I'm glad you stopped by, Sam. I need someone to help me test the sound system."

"Tell me again why it is we need a sound system?"

"For the commercials for Clevis Nagle. I talked him into donating half the cost toward renting the sound system."

"Will we be doing anything else with the sound system? Perhaps playing music or Scripture readings?"

"Nope, just the commercials for the movie theater," Dale said. "That was part of the deal if Clevis paid half of it."

I thought about that for a moment. "Now, Dale, I might be mistaken, and please correct me if I'm wrong, but it seems to me that if Clevis only paid half, and his commercials are the only thing we're using the sound system for, then we're paying Clevis money so we can advertise for him."

"Well, I suppose if you wanna be pessimistic, you can look at it that way. But he didn't have to pay any of it at all. Then we wouldna even had a sound system. This way, we have the only Nativity scene in town with a sound system." He beamed at the thought of it.

It had been a long day, and I was tired. Plus, the goose was thrashing around in the trunk of my car, so I let the matter drop.

When I arrived home, I put the goose in the garage and removed the duct tape from his beak, receiving a peck on the head for my troubles. I went in the side door to the kitchen. My wife was standing at the sink washing the supper dishes. "How's our goose?" she asked.

"All tucked into bed." I picked up a dish towel and began to dry and put away.

"How long will those animals be in our garage?"

"Just until the twenty-eighth, but no later than the thirtieth."

She sagged at the sink. "I could smell them during dinner."

"Maybe we could start eating in the dining room," I suggested.

"Tell me again why we're doing a Nativity scene this year."

"It's easier," I said.

"For whom is it easier?"

The secret of marital longevity is knowing when to change the subject. "How about guessing what I got you for Christmas," I suggested.

"Not livestock, I hope."

"No, not livestock."

"Jewelry?"

"No, it turns you green. Remember?"

"Not all of it turns me green."

I told her I didn't want to risk it.

"What I could use is a new toaster," she said, turning toward me and smiling.

I grimaced. "I don't know. They're pretty expensive. You think you've been good enough this year?"

"I'm putting up with your livestock, aren't I?"

I was glad I had splurged and bought the four-slotter.

Off in the distance, toward the Asa Peacock farm, I could hear the occasional bark of gunfire.

"Sounds like Dale is up late tonight," Barbara observed.

"Sounds like it."

"I wonder if he got many volunteers."

"I know Bea volunteered, and Fern Hampton's nephew, Ervin."

"I feel safer already."

It was late. Now that we were feeding livestock, we'd have to rise early. I was lying in bed, waiting for Barbara to finish in the bathroom so I could brush my teeth when I heard a thunderous BOOM! I raised up out of bed and peered through the window. There was a faint orange glow on the horizon.

"What was that?" Barbara called out from the bathroom.

"I'm not exactly sure." I pulled on my pants and shirt and walked toward the door, with Barbara right behind me. Just then the high wail of the fire station alarm split the evening air. We hurried out into the front yard. Up and down the street, I saw lights flickering on and people coming out of their houses to stare at the sky.

Barbara reached over and took my hand, her face tight with concern. "What do you suppose is happening?" she asked again.

"I'm not sure. But whatever it is, it can't be good."

$Seven$

The Progressive

Whoen I arrived at the meetinghouse the day before Christmas Eve, Dale Hinshaw and Asa Peacock were waiting in my office.

"It's not my fault," Dale said, as I came through the door. "You shoulda told us you were coming. It wasn't my fault it blew up."

"What blew up?" I asked, wading into the conversation at midstream.

"My pickup truck," Asa moaned. "I heard shooting in my back field last night. I thought it was hunters. When I went to run 'em off, Dale shot at me and hit the gas tank. I barely got out before the truck exploded."

Dale reddened. "Well, what did you expect? It was pitch black. How could I know it was you? Besides, you said we could use your field for our security training."

"You didn't tell me you were going to be out there at night," Asa complained.

"Will someone please tell me what this has to do with our church?" I asked.

"Dale said the church'll buy me another truck, since they were there on church business," Asa explained.

"Wasn't your truck insured?"

Asa glared at Dale. "Try telling that to Dale. He's my insurance agent, but he said this type of thing isn't covered, that the church has to pay for it."

I stared at Dale. "Let me get this right. You blew up Asa's truck and you expect the church to pay for it?"

Dale shrugged and looked helpless, as if the matter were out of his hands. "Asa's policy doesn't cover acts of war."

One more day, and it would all be over. Dale would be gone to his sister-in-law's house a hundred miles away. The progressive Nativity scene would be done with, at least for another year.

"Dale, the church didn't ask you to provide security for the Nativity scene. That was your idea. Now you've blown up Asa's truck. You're his insurance agent, so you figure out a way to pay him for his truck." I spoke slowly so he would understand.

"I want a 1968 red Ford," Asa said. "Just like I had."

"Asa, can't you see I got more important things to worry about just now?" Dale said. He turned toward me. "Ned Kivett wants his angel of the Lord back. We can't have a Nativity scene without an angel of the Lord. I was thinkin' maybe I could borrow one of your boys."

"Borrow one of my boys? What would you do with him?"

"Dangle him from a branch over the manger. It'll only be for a couple hours. He can wear long underwear so he don't get cold. All he has to do is yell, 'Glory to God in the highest!' every now and then."

"I don't think so, Dale. Why don't you make an angel of the Lord out of plywood like the Baptist church?"

He frowned. "That won't do. Dang that Ned Kivett anyway."

"I would love for you to stay and visit," I lied, "but I have work to do."

I ushered them to the door, said my good-byes, told Frank not to let anyone in, then locked my office door and lay down on the couch in my office—an unsold remnant from a church rummage sale years before. I could feel a throbbing pain start at the back of my head, move over my scalp, and center itself between my eyes. A Dale migraine.

Twenty years before, I had sat in this very office and confided in Pastor Taylor that I wanted to be a minister, having mistaken Miriam Hodge's compliment on my Youth Sunday sermon as a sign of God's call. Now it was too late. I was tied to the tracks and the progressive Nativity scene was steaming toward me—my punishment for taking the wrong path in life.

Pastor Taylor had suggested I find another vocation and volunteer in the church instead. "You don't want to do this," he'd said. "Your life isn't your own, and the pay's lousy. People hound you all the time. Why don't you get a normal job and volunteer in the church. You don't have to be a pastor."

But I was young and pigheaded and couldn't be dissuaded. In arrogance born of youthfulness, I presumed I would be a better pastor than Pastor Taylor and could easily master the challenges that had discouraged him. I hadn't counted on Dale Hinshaw.

I knocked off at noontime to eat lunch with Frank at the Coffee Cup. It was more crowded than usual, the farmers having come to town to buy Christmas gifts for their wives. We had to sit on stools at the counter, beside the Juicy Fruit rack next to the cash register. Large, pear-shaped men lined up behind me to pay their bills. I spent my lunch craning my neck around to answer their questions. "Yes, I'm fine. She's fine, too." "No, I hadn't heard that joke. I'll have to remember it." "Last Sunday's offering was fine, thank you, did you want to add to it?" That usually silenced them.

There were a few comments about the progressive Nativity scene. Didn't we think ten dollars was too much? Why had Dale shot at Asa? Would he be shooting anyone else? Was it safe to take their children? I assured them the money was going for a good cause, Brother Norman's shoe ministry to the Choctaw Indians, and that we had told Dale not to bring his gun.

Then Frank and I discussed our Christmas plans. He was going to help me with the livestock, then hit the sack, wake up early, and call his daughter and granddaughter in North Carolina.

"You could be down there by midnight if you left now," I said. "The roads are clear. Why not go be with your family?"

"They didn't invite me. Besides, they're leaving for vacation to Florida on Christmas afternoon. Plus, who'd help you with the livestock?"

"There's not much livestock left," I said. "Barbara loaded the pigs in the car and took them back to Ellis and Miriam's. She said Jewish people wouldn't have had pigs anyway. I guess Dale hadn't thought of that. Now we're down to a cow, a sheep, and a goose."

"Do you know none of the Gospels mention any animals at the birth of Jesus?"

"I know that, and you know that, but don't tell Dale. He'll get all worked up."

"And according to the Gospel of Matthew, the wise men didn't show up until two years later," Frank observed. "Did you know that?"

"Yes, but don't say anything to Bea. She's been sewing wise men costumes all week."

"Did you know Mark's Gospel doesn't even mention Jesus' birth, and that most scholars consider it the most accurate Gospel?" he asked.

I looked at him. My eyes narrowed in suspicion. "Frank, have you been reading my *Progressive Christianity* magazine again?"

"It was on top of your desk. Besides, if you don't want people knowing you read those kind of magazines, you need to hide them under your mattress."

Penny came to take our dishes away. "Not meaning to be rude, but it is Christmas Eve and some people would like to get home early. Like me, for instance, so could you two move along, for crying out loud?"

We settled up our bill, then went our separate ways,

Frank to his house and me to mine. I kept our sons occupied while Barbara hid out in the bedroom wrapping Christmas presents. Even though we were down to three animals, it took several hours to groom them. Except for the goose, who was opposed to grooming, and pecked me on the head when I tried to brush him. That was fine with me. If he wanted to go out in public looking like a mess, that was his business.

Frank came for supper, then we herded our menagerie out to the front yard for the livestock portion of the progressive Nativity scene. It was already dark. We'd no sooner staked out the animals than Bob Miles from the *Herald* stopped to take a picture. "You're the second stop. I just came from Dale's. Boy, he's got some setup over there. Signs and lights and Clevis Nagle running the sound system. How Dale ever got his wife up in that tree, I'll never know."

"His wife?"

"Yep, she's supposed to be the angel of the Lord. But I think they've had a fight. He told her she needed to look more joyful, and she told him, well, maybe I better not say what she told him. Anyway, she didn't look too happy."

He pulled his camera from his bag. "Sam, if you could, why don't you stand next to the animals so I can get your picture. I'll make sure you get some extra copies to send to your relatives out of town."

"No thank you, Bob. I'd rather they never found out about this."

He snapped a dozen pictures before moving on to Asa and Jessie Peacock's house to view the Holy Family.

By now I was anxious to visit the other stops. I asked Frank to hold down the fort while I traveled the progressive Nativity circuit. Dale's house was closest, so I went there first. I wasn't expecting much, so I was surprised to see cars lining both sides of the street for several blocks in each direction. It looked as though everyone in town was there. I had to park three blocks away. I hung back from the crowd, not wanting to be publicly identified with this event, trying to appear as if I were from out of town and had wandered past by accident.

The sound of static filled the air, then the clearing of a throat, and Clevis Nagle came on the sound system. "Welcome to the Progressive Nativity Scene of Harmony Friends Meeting, sound system compliments of Clevis Nagle and the Royal Theater. We'll be closed this week, but will reopen the day after Christmas with a showing of *Santa Claws!* See what happens when an escaped grizzly dismembers a mid-Western family on Christmas Eve! As usual, family discounts are available. So bring the kids for an unforgettable evening of holiday fun!"

Dale stood off to the side, beaming.

I had seen enough. I walked back to my car, then drove out to the country to Asa and Jessie's house to see the Holy Family. There was no one there, except for Asa and Jessie in bathrobes, who looked a little long in the tooth to be with child. They were clustered around the Baby Jesus, compliments of Kivett's Five and Dime. Behind them, in the barnyard, I could see the blackened husk of Asa's truck.

I climbed from the car. We exchanged pleasantries. "Been busy?" I asked.

"Not a soul's been by," Asa said.

"Everyone's over at Dale's," I said. "They'll be by before long."

We visited for a while, but still no one came, so I left for Bea's house. No one was there either, except for three wise men—Ellis Hodge, Fern's nephew Ervin, and the radio man from WEAK, who appeared to be giving serious thought to finding another line of work. They were huddled around a small fire, rubbing their hands briskly, while also trying to look reverent as they worshiped the Baby Jesus, which was no small trick since he was three miles away in Asa's front yard.

I asked if anyone had stopped by.

"Not a soul," they reported.

This was worse than the Christmas the year of Pastor Taylor's midlife crisis, when he'd read from the California Bible.

I pushed on to Fern's house, not looking forward to facing thirty irate Friendly Women. But, to my surprise, it was packed. The cookie sales were brisk, Fern reported happily. Apparently, people had decided to skip Jesus and go straight to the refreshments. Not an altogether uncommon occurrence.

I visited briefly with the ladies of the Circle, drank some hot chocolate, then took half a dozen cookies back to Frank. No one had stopped by. "I don't think they're getting it," he said. "I don't think people understood they were supposed to come by here next."

"They're over at Fern's eating cookies," I explained. "Asa and Jessie didn't have anyone stop by either."

"Mind if I go home?" he asked.

"No, go ahead. And thanks for your help, Frank. I appreciate it."

"Need some help getting the animals in?"

"No, I can handle it."

We waved good-bye, and then I led the animals back to the garage.

My boys were still up, but in their pajamas, so I read them a story, answered their barrage of questions, then tucked them in. Barbara was downstairs arranging their presents under the tree. I was too preoccupied to sleep, so I decided to go for a walk.

I headed toward town, past Dale's house. The people were gone, and Dale was taking down the sound system. I hoped in the dark he wouldn't notice me, but he did. "What a night that was," he said. "Wasn't that something?"

"It certainly was something," I agreed.

"Did you get by the Peacocks' house?" he asked.

"Yes, I did."

Dale paused for a moment, and a thoughtful look crossed his face. Never having seen Dale look thoughtful, I was caught off guard.

"You know, Sam, having the Nativity scene spread out like that kinda reminded me how we never really see the full picture. We think we do, but mostly we're just lookin' at bits and pieces, thinkin' we're seeing the whole thing."

I was utterly stunned at his insight.

"Say," Dale said, "this was such a hit, why don't we be thinkin' about doing something like this for Easter? Maybe have a Crucifixion in my yard and the Resurrection in your yard. Wouldn't that be something?"

It appeared Dale's detour into wisdom would be a brief one.

"I guess it's something to think about," I said. "Well, Dale, you take care. Safe travels to your sister-in-law's."

I continued walking toward town. Before long, I could see the Christmas lights the Odd Fellows had strung across Main Street. It was late and still, except for an occasional car driving by. I walked past the meetinghouse and noticed Frank had left a light on, so I went in to turn it off. Frank was there, seated by himself in the third pew, right-hand side.

I wasn't going to disturb him, but he looked up, noticed me, and motioned for me to sit beside him.

"Hey, Frank."

"Hey, Sam."

"Everything all right?"

"Oh, sure. I don't know. I was just walking past and thought I'd sit for a while. It's nice in here."

"Yes, it is," I agreed. "Very peaceful."

"So I'm sitting here thinking old-man thoughts."

I didn't know what to say, so I kept quiet.

"Mostly remembering when my daughter was little and we'd sit here on Christmas Eve. She'd be in her pajamas. Right here." He patted his lap. "Now she's in North Carolina. I wonder how she is."

"I'm sure she's just fine," I said.

He didn't speak for several moments. "I missed this tonight. I missed the Gospel of Luke and going to the basement for cookies."

"I did, too, Frank. I missed it, too."

We grew quiet, remembering. Frank with his Yule thoughts, and me with mine. Sitting at the dining-room table writing out Christmas cards with my wife. Walking the aisles of the Five and Dime searching for the perfect gift, my sons in tow. Finding that exquisite tree at Grant's Hardware, eight feet tall with vertical integrity, a tree among trees. Watching Clarence the angel rescue George Bailey on a Friday night at the Royal. My boys sitting on Santa's lap— one a skeptic, the other a true believer. Tucking them in bed not an hour before, their little bodies squirming with excitement. Still little, and still with me, and not in North Carolina. Not even the prospect of Dale's progressive Easter could dampen that.

I heard a slight sniff and came out of my reverie. "Uh, Sam, I was wondering if you could maybe do me a favor?"

"Sure, Frank, what is it?"

"I was hoping maybe you could you read the second chapter of Luke for me. Not the whole thing, just the birth part."

"Yeah, I can do that." I reached for a pew Bible.

"No, Sam, not here. Could you read it from the pulpit, like we've always done?"

I walked up to the pulpit, opened the pulpit Bible to the Gospel of Luke, and began to read. Frank closed his eyes and tilted his head back, letting the words wash over him. "And it came to pass in those days, that there went out a decree from Caesar Augustus that all the world should be taxed. . . . And she brought forth her firstborn son, and wrapped him in swaddling clothes, and laid him in a manger, because there was no room for them in the inn . . . Fear not: for, behold, I bring you good tidings of great joy, which shall be to all people."

I closed the Bible and sat back down next to Frank. He reached in his coat pocket and pulled out the cookies I had given him earlier. "Care for a cookie?" he asked.

"Thank you, Frank. Don't mind if I do."

We sat like that until the Frieda Hampton memorial clock bonged midnight.

"Merry Christmas, Sam."

"Merry Christmas to you, Frank."

The stream of some forty Christmas Eves in that place now blend into one, except for that year, which I've never told anyone about until now, trusting you will not think me foolish for believing it to be perhaps my finest Christmas eve.

If you would like to correspond directly with Philip Gulley, please send mail to:

Philip Gulley
c/o HarperSanFrancisco
353 Sacramento Street
Suite 500
San Francisco, CA 94111

In addition to writing, Philip Gulley also enjoys the ministry of speaking. If you would like more information, please contact:

David Leonards
3612 North Washington Boulevard
Indianapolis, IN 46205–3592
317–926–7566
ieb@prodigy.net

ALSO BY PHILIP GULLEY

Nonfiction
Front Porch Tales
Hometown Tales
For Everything a Season

Fiction
Home to Harmony
Just Shy of Harmony

Coming Spring 2003
Signs and Wonders: A Harmony Novel

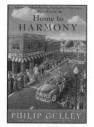
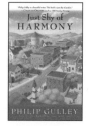
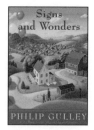